THE
COLD, COLD
SHOULDER

Anne Schraff

PAGETURNERS

SUSPENSE
Boneyard
The Cold, Cold Shoulder
The Girl Who Had Everything
Hamlet's Trap
Roses Red as Blood

DETECTIVE
The Case of the Bad Seed
The Case of the Cursed Chalet
The Case of the Dead Duck
The Case of the Wanted Man
The Case of the Watery Grave

ADVENTURE
A Horse Called Courage
Planet Doom
The Terrible Orchid Sky
Up Rattler Mountain
Who Has Seen the Beast?

SCIENCE FICTION
Bugged!
Escape from Earth
Flashback
Murray's Nightmare
Under Siege

MYSTERY
The Hunter
Once Upon a Crime
Whatever Happened to
  Megan Marie?
When Sleeping Dogs Awaken
Where's Dudley?

SPY
A Deadly Game
An Eye for an Eye
I Spy, e-Spy
Scavenger Hunt
Tuesday Raven

Development and Production: Laurel Associates, Inc.
Cover and Interior Art: Black Eagle Productions

SADDLEBACK
PUBLISHING·INC.
Three Watson
Irvine, CA 92618-2767
E-Mail: info@sdlback.com
Website: www.sdlback.com

ISBN 1-56254-701-1

Printed in the United States of America

09 08 07 06 05 04   9 8 7 6 5 4 3 2 1

CONTENTS

Chapter 1

The big rooming house on Caufield Lane reminded Cody Walker of the house that he'd lived in for much of his childhood. More than 100 years old, Grandmother's three-story house was surrounded by an old apple orchard, still bearing fruit. That comfortable home had sheltered several generations of the Walker family—but eight strangers lived in this house on Caufield Lane. Some were college students, while others, like Cody, worked at the new discount department store in town.

At 20, Cody was already a rolling stone. Before working as a clerk at the department store, he'd been a tree trimmer and a mechanic's helper, among other things. Cody's parents had died when he was a small boy. After his grandmother died, he had spent several years in the foster care system. When he'd turned 18, he left Los Angeles and hit the road. The road had brought him to Pioneer Lake just last summer.

Cody didn't make friends easily, but he did hang out with another young guy at the rooming house. Like Cody, Todd Clifford worked at the department store. The boys jogged together and sometimes went fishing or hung out at one of the local night spots.

The two young men made fun of the college students by calling them "bookheads." Cody and Todd were high school dropouts. The truth was that they were envious of the college kids.

"Did you see Freddy Paine leaving for school this morning?" Cody asked Todd one morning. "I heard him clicking away on his computer last night."

Todd shook his head. "No, I didn't.

Maybe he studied so hard he collapsed of exhaustion onto his mouse," he laughed.

A sour-faced middle-aged man, Red Breck, managed the rooming house. He said he was a widower whose children were grown and gone.

Now, as Cody and Todd walked toward the car, they passed Breck. "Did you happen to see Freddy Paine this morning?" Cody asked. "Maybe he overslept. Man, if he was late for school, he must have had a fit!"

Breck shrugged. "That's his problem. It's not my job to get the tenants out of bed in the morning," he said grumpily.

As Cody started to back his car out of the driveway, Todd spotted Ashley Root, another college student, hurrying toward the bus stop. "Hold up," Todd said to Cody. Then he leaned out the window and called out to Ashley. "Hey, Ash! Want a lift to school?"

"Yeah, sure," she said. "It beats waiting for the stupid bus."

Todd hopped out and held the door open for her. "You go ahead and take the front seat, Ash. I'll get in the back."

Without so much as a thank-you to Todd, Ashley took his place. Cody turned toward her. "Ash, did you see Freddy Paine this morning? He's usually biked halfway to school by now."

"I don't pay any attention to the slugs who live here," Ashley said with a yawn.

When they'd moved in, both Cody and Todd had noticed Ashley right away. She was by far the best-looking girl here. But for some reason she seemed to hate boys.

Cody had started to back up the car again, but then he suddenly put on the brakes. "You know, maybe I'd better check on Freddy. It'll only take a minute," he said as he hopped out of the car.

Ashley groaned. "Oh, give me a break!" she said, rolling her eyes.

Cody sprinted back to the rooming house and went up to Freddy's room.

He was about to knock when he noticed that the door was slightly ajar.

The rumpled bed was empty. Freddy's backpack was on the floor. The only thing amiss in the room was the clock radio. It had fallen on the floor. It looked like Freddy had left in a hurry. The time on the clock had stopped at 12:10 A.M.

What had happened? The scene didn't look a bit like Freddy. The guy was a neat freak. Under normal circumstances Freddy's room gave Cody the guilts about his own sloppiness. Cody had always thought that if the fire alarm went off some night, Freddy would tidy up before he tried to escape. He would *never* leave a rumpled bed behind.

Cody was worried. Even though Freddy Paine was a college student and all, Cody felt bad for him. The guy was kind of shy and geeky, and he seemed to be pretty lonely.

Hey, Freddy, what's going on? Cody said to himself. *You didn't make your bed, man.*

9

What's up with that, dude? Where'd you go?

Then, from outside, Cody heard Ashley complaining to Todd.

"Where is he? We've got to get going!" Then she started yelling out the car window. "Cody! Come on out of there! What are you doing? I can't be late for Miss Crabapple's class. She'd just love to flunk me for being late! *Cody!*"

Cody sighed as he glanced around the room one more time. Then he headed out to the car, shaking his head. He couldn't shake an uneasy feeling that something had happened to poor Freddy Paine. Cody got those intuitions sometimes— and mostly they panned out.

Chapter 2

"So, did he oversleep?" Todd asked when Cody climbed back in the car.

"Nah, he wasn't even there. Looks like he left in a hurry at 12:10 A.M. That's when he must have knocked over his clock radio. He didn't even bother to pick it up," Cody said.

"So what? Can we get going now?" Ashley snapped. "I'll be late for class! My math teacher is a mean old witch. She crawls all over people for being late."

As Cody drove toward the campus and the department store, he couldn't get Freddy off his mind. The guy was so *meticulous*. He couldn't imagine him tearing out of his room at 12:10 A.M. and leaving his busted radio on the floor.

"I figure something really wild must have happened to Freddy. Maybe he got a bad phone call or something," Cody said.

"Yeah—like anybody cares," Ashley grumbled. "He's a freak! Always staring at me. He gives me the creeps!"

"He's not a bad guy," Cody said. He was constantly surprised by what a rotten personality Ashley had. He pitied the poor fool who might marry her one day.

"Too bad I have to go to a community college," Ashley said. "I wanted to go to an ivy league school. But my parents are losers. They can't afford it."

It's all about you, isn't it, Ash? Cody thought to himself.

"You're a pretty good student. Can't you get a scholarship?" Todd asked her.

"Maybe—but not enough to cover everything. Boy, I never have any luck," Ashley said bitterly.

Cody dropped off Ashley at the northwest corner of the campus. She jumped from the car and hurried off—

once again, without even a thank-you.

"What a winner she is!" Cody said sarcastically. "Talk about losers, she sure got missed when they were passing out personality."

Todd shook his head. "Yeah, but she's *so* beautiful," he said. "I get weak in the knees just looking at her."

"Nah, she's a creep," Cody said. "My grandmother always said, 'Beauty is as beauty does.' That always stuck with me. I'll never fall for a girl unless she's nice."

"Guess you're right," Todd said half-heartedly, still looking after Ashley as she ran across the campus.

"Ashley's like a great-looking apple with a big, fat worm in it," Cody went on. "The worm is her stinky attitude. She doesn't even care what happened to Freddy! We're not really friends, but we all live under the same roof! I'd like to know what happened."

"Freddy is such a little weirdo," Todd said. "Don't worry about him. He probably remembered reading about a big meteor shower at 12:15. Then he leaped out of bed to see it and—"

"Where is he now, though?" Cody asked. "He'd never skip school."

They pulled into the employees' parking lot and went in to work. Cody didn't enjoy his job. There were always mobs of people waiting at the checkout stands. Some of them got really angry and impatient. The store was too cheap to hire enough checkers, so the customers took out their frustration on the clerks who were there.

Sometimes Cody wondered if he should be a "bookhead," too. He could squeeze in a couple of college classes if he tried. Otherwise, he might end up like his father, who'd still been a roofer's helper at the age of 45. Then one day he fell off a roof and broke his neck, leaving a wife and four kids. Cody's mother had faded away and died shortly after his father's death. Cody had always thought the trauma of it all must have been too much for her. Since then, Cody had lost track of his older brother and sisters.

Cody sighed. It would be horrible if he were still here at the checkout counter 5 or 10 years from now.

When he got back home in the late afternoon, the first thing Cody did was check Freddy's room. Everything was just as it had been that morning. The broken clock radio was still on the floor.

Cody tracked down Red Breck. "Look, I think something bad might have happened to Freddie Paine," he said.

Breck followed Cody upstairs, and they both went in Freddy's room.

"What do you think? Where could the guy be?" Cody asked.

"Like I should know," Breck snapped. "We'll wait a couple days. If he's not back then, I'll clean the room and rent it to somebody else. The rent is due day after tomorrow, you know. If he doesn't show up, I'll just throw his stuff in a box and toss it out with the rest of the trash."

Cody couldn't believe his ears. "But don't you think we should call the police?" he asked. "I mean, obviously, Red, *something* has happened to the guy."

Chapter 3

"Call the *police*?" Breck's sandpapery voice exploded. "Are you nuts? These kids are like leaves. They blow in and out with every little gust of wind. I've been here too long to be surprised when one of them just takes off without a word. The truth is, *I don't care* what happened with Paine. It's none of my business."

"But, shouldn't you call Freddy's family or something?" Cody asked.

"Kid, I'm not a nanny, okay? *You* call them if you're so worried. It's not my job to wet nurse a bunch of punks," Breck said over his shoulder as he stomped off.

Cody stood there, staring into the empty room. He had no idea whether or not Freddy had a family. Cody knew that if anything happened to him, there would be no family to call. It had been more than five years since Cody's last contact with his brother. Maybe Freddy had the same kind of situation.

Keri Alvarez, who lived in the room across from Freddy, peeked out her door. She was a college girl, too—cute, but not drop-dead beautiful like Ashley.

"What's going on, Cody?" she asked.

"Freddy's been missing since late last night. Did you see him go somewhere?" Cody asked the girl.

"Just after midnight I heard voices in the hall. I was half-asleep, so I couldn't tell you who they were. Then I heard something that sounded like a scuffle. After that somebody seemed to be hauling a really heavy garbage bag or something downstairs. I heard it thumping on the stairs. Then everything was quiet again," Keri said.

"Did you see Freddy?" Cody asked.

"No. I didn't even get out of bed,"

Keri said. Now she looked a bit worried.

"Well, he's gone. His bike is in the garage, and his backpack is lying on the floor," Cody said.

"Did you call his dad?" Keri asked. "Maybe he's gone home. Maybe he got a call that there's an illness in the family or something, so he left in a hurry."

"I didn't even know he had a family," Cody said. "Do you happen to have his dad's number or address?"

Keri shook her head. "Freddy and I went for coffee once, and he told me his dad lives somewhere on the west coast. He said he'd gone to live with his dad after his parents got divorced. But when his dad remarried, he moved out on his own. I don't know anything more than that," she said.

Cody was surprised that Freddy had gone out with Keri. He seemed like such a shy guy.

"So, did you guys date or something?" Cody asked.

Keri laughed a little. "Oh, no. It wasn't a date. Actually, I'm sort of friends with Ashley Root. Freddy had a big crush on *her*. He wanted advice on how to get her to go out with him," she said.

"No kidding," Cody marveled. Freddy was kind of prissy and sort of weird-looking. How could he imagine that a girl like Ashley Root would go for him? She wasn't even civil to good-looking guys.

"Yeah. Poor Freddy," Keri said. "I guess he thought Ashley and I were really close. But actually, we just have a couple classes together, and once in a while we go to the gym. I'm afraid I wasn't much help to him. I'm sure that *I* don't know the secret to Ashley's heart!"

"Ha!" Cody laughed. "The secret is that she *has* no heart!"

Keri came across the hall and joined Cody in Freddy's room.

"What's that?" Keri said, pointing to a stain on the rug. Cody's mouth dropped open. He hadn't even noticed it before.

"I don't know. It almost looks like, uh—blood, doesn't it?" Cody said.

Keri gaped. "I guess it could be catsup or maybe grape juice," she said in a suddenly queasy voice.

"Look, Keri, Freddy's clock radio is on the floor, busted. He must have been surprised by someone. . . ." Cody's voice trailed away.

Keri looked worried. "Maybe there was a fight," she added. "Oh, Cody, did you tell Mr. Breck about this? I think he should call the police."

"I already talked to him. He doesn't want to be bothered," Cody said.

Keri looked scared. "But if a prowler surprised Freddy and hurt him—I mean we could *all* be in danger."

"Yeah, we need to call the police even if Breck won't," Cody said. He hurried to his room and dialed 911. He told the dispatcher that someone was missing and there was a stain that looked like blood on the floor of his room.

Cody wondered if Freddy Paine had another life—a secret life. People could be like that sometimes. It surprised him that Freddy had thought about dating Ashley. Maybe he wasn't the guy he seemed to be.

Whenever Freddy tried to act cool, it came off really bad. Once he had tried to join in on a conversation about drugs with some of the other roomers. Freddy had tried to pretend he knew all about the drug scene. But it was clear he didn't know what he was talking about. The other guys had laughed at him.

Then, without quite knowing why, Cody thought about the day his brother Bucky took him hunting. Cody had never cared much for the sport because it didn't seem fair. Most of the animals seemed pretty stupid—like the rabbits that just stood still when they heard you coming. But that day Cody had gone along with his brother. Bucky was horsing around shooting all over the woods.

Then a man screamed.

Cody was terrified. To him it was pretty obvious what had happened. Bucky had accidentally shot another hunter!

"We gotta go find that guy right now, Bucky," Cody had said. "He's hurt and may be dying."

Bucky got a wild look in his eyes, a look that Cody had never seen before. "No—we gotta run," he gasped.

He grabbed Cody by the shirt and dragged him away. After walking for half an hour, Bucky threw his rifle into a deep ravine. Then he bent over and screamed in Cody's face, "Don't you ever tell anybody what happened, or I'll wring your neck!"

Before that, Cody had looked up to Bucky as a hero. But now he knew better. Later, they heard that the wounded hunter had survived. Nobody ever knew who had shot him. When Bucky disappeared the following summer, Cody was glad.

It occurred to Cody that Freddy's past might be similar to his own. Maybe there were dark secrets in the little guy's life. But what could have caused him to leap out of bed and smash his clock radio and just disappear? Maybe he'd cut his foot on a little piece of glass and left that blood—

Where are the cops? Cody wondered.

Then he noticed Red Breck heading for his old pickup truck. Cody had never liked the cranky rooming house manager. In fact, he got the creeps just looking at the man.

Chapter 4

As Cody waited for the police to arrive, he wondered if Red Breck might have had anything to do with Freddy's disappearance. Breck had the nosy habit of going into the tenants' rooms when they were out. He always said he needed to tidy up—but once ten dollars had gone missing from Cody's desk drawer. And Ashley had complained that her watch had mysteriously disappeared.

Maybe Breck had gone into the room while Freddy was asleep and started rummaging through his bookbag. And maybe Freddy woke up and the two of them had fought. Breck might have hit him too hard and killed him. Breck was six foot three, and he weighed about 230.

It would have been easy for him to stick little Freddy in a garbage bag and drag him down the stairs.

Red Breck was furious when the police arrived. He glared at Cody and angrily stated that no one but he had the right to get the police involved.

As the officers took pictures and searched the room, Breck stood by with another tenant, Louis Denham. He was older than the other roomers, kind of a drifter handyman—with a drinking problem. Breck gave him a break on his rent in exchange for light maintenance. Denham could fix most electrical or plumbing problems.

Now Louis walked up to one of the officers and said, "I know what happened to the guy."

The young police officer nodded. "Okay, let's have it," he said.

"Last night I heard this ruckus up in Paine's room. I could hear the kid freaking out inside, so I knocked on the door and went in. The kid must have been on drugs or something. He'd cut himself, and he was bleeding. That must be how that bloodstain got on the rug. I offered to take him to the emergency room to get stitched up, but he wouldn't hear of it. The next thing I knew, he was stumbling down the stairs and walked out toward the orchard. That's the last I saw of him," Denham said.

"No way!" Cody cried out. "Freddy Paine never touched drugs."

Denham looked hard at Cody. He was a big guy, like Breck.

"Well, he was on *something* when I saw him. I swear he was as high as a kite on a windy day," he growled.

"Yeah, I've seen him freaking out before," Breck said. "You can ask Ashley Root. She came to me and complained that he was harassing her."

Breck's and Denham's stories took the steam out of the police investigation. Now they had a plausible explanation for

Freddy Paine's disappearance and the blood on the carpet. Same old, same old: Just another young guy losing it under the influence of some drug. For all they knew, he might still be wandering around in the apple orchard.

When the police left, Breck told Cody that he'd better mind his own business in the future. If the police needed to be called, he'd take care of it. Then Breck ordered Denham to clean out Freddy's room the next morning.

"I don't need this kind of grief," Breck complained. "And it gives the rooming house a bad name."

On his way back to his own room, Cody rapped on Ashley's door. He couldn't believe that a timid guy like Freddy had actually harassed her.

Ashley was perspiring heavily when she came to the door. She kept gym equipment in the room and worked hard at keeping in shape. Yet even glossy with sweat, her dark hair damp and frizzy, she still looked stunningly beautiful.

"Ashley, I don't want to bother you, but we need to talk. Red Breck said you complained to him that Freddy Paine was harassing you. That just doesn't seem possible. Not Freddy."

"Yeah, he was," Ashley said. "The slobbering little creep. He was always lurking around, trying to see what he could see. I told him to get lost, but he didn't get the message. I almost had to laugh, though. To think I'd give a little freak like him a second look!"

Cody hid the disgust he was feeling. Ashley was always strutting around in skimpy little outfits. If she didn't want attention, what was that all about?

"Who *would* be worth a second look, Ashley?" Cody asked. "Just out of curiosity, I'd like to know."

Ashley sneered at him. "Don't go there, Cody. Don't even try to go there. You haven't got a chance."

Ashley tossed her head and said, "You

know something, Cody, there are very few people in this freaky world who are really *tens*. You know where I'm coming from? Tens have gotta have good bones and great bods. Like me. Most guys I run into are like *fives* at the most. Freddy, he was a two—maybe. One-and-a-half is closer to the mark. It's really insulting to be hit on by a guy who's a one-and-a-half."

Cody was disgusted. "You've got a wonderful way with words, Ashley. But if you ever enter the Miss Beautiful Girl contest, you'll never be picked for Miss Congeniality," he said.

"Like I care," Ashley said. "I've got too much to do to waste my time buttering up losers. But don't feel too bad, Cody. You're way better than Freddy. I mean your hair is awful, but you could get it styled. And you need to dress better. You look like you just dropped off a farm truck or something. Do you have any idea what the cool guys are wearing these days?"

"Gosh, no—long, dangly earrings?" Cody asked in a snide voice.

"Sometimes. But, like I was saying, You have some possibilities if you'd work at it. Not that *I'd* ever want to go out with you. I mean, not unless you and I were stranded on a desert island and I was totally out-of-my-gourd desperate," Ashley said with a laugh.

Cody had had enough. "Did anyone ever tell you that you're a real witch?" he asked.

Ashley glared at him for a minute. Then she said coldly, "Don't mess with me, Cody. You're way out of your league." Then she closed the door in his face.

Chapter 5

Cody stood outside her door for a minute. He was sorry he hadn't had a chance to tell her that he wouldn't take her out if she was the last woman on earth.

Cody didn't believe Louis Denham's story. Clearly, that was just something he'd cooked up at Red Breck's urging. Another favor for the boss. Why was Breck so anxious to get rid of the police? Maybe he *did* have something to do with Freddy's disappearance. Or maybe he simply didn't want to be bothered.

Cody didn't have to work the next morning, so he decided to take a walk in the apple orchard. He'd reluctantly come to the conclusion that Freddy Paine might be dead. Maybe whoever had killed him had buried him out there. Cody wanted to look for freshly turned earth.

Hey, dude, it's not really your business, Cody reminded himself. But for some reason, he couldn't forget it. Freddy Paine wasn't a bad guy. He had his whole life ahead of him. Like everybody else, the guy had his dreams. One time he'd said he wanted to be an astronomer. He didn't deserve to be shoved off the planet at age 21.

Cody had learned a lot while living with his grandmother. She'd always been available to lend a hand when there was trouble in the neighborhood. He'd often seen her calming battling spouses, comforting children, consoling the bereaved, and making casseroles for those left behind. Cody's grandmother had *cared* about people—and that was her gift to him. The more he thought about it, the more Cody felt he had an obligation to get justice for Freddy.

If the poor kid was dead, there was a murderer out there. It wasn't fair to Freddy to just let the guy go.

"Hey, man," Todd said, catching up to Cody at the edge of the orchard, "It's our day off! I thought we'd go fishing. What are you doing out here?"

"If you really want to know, I'm hunting for a grave, Todd," Cody said.

Todd paled. "You mean *Freddy*? You really think he's dead?"

"Maybe. And *for sure* Red Breck and Denham cooked up that phony story about Freddy freaking out. They told the cops Freddy went nuts and cut himself and then ran off into the woods. But that doesn't hold water. I think either Breck or Denham might have killed the poor guy. Maybe they were poking around in his room looking for something to steal and Freddy confronted them," Cody said.

Todd shuddered. "But I can't believe they're murderers," he said. "I mean, they look like just regular guys."

"What do murderers look like?" Cody asked. "Do they have horns coming out of the top of their heads? Do they have forked tongues? Get real, buddy. They look like everybody else."

"But Cody, the cops were here, and they looked around," Todd said.

"They didn't look very thoroughly. Denham's story let them off easy. They figured Freddy just went bonkers on some drug and that he'd come back eventually," Cody said.

Just then, they heard the sound of pounding feet. Ashley Root and Keri Alvarez were jogging through the orchard. Keri wore a baggy sweatshirt, but, as usual, Ashley was wearing a skintight tanktop and short shorts.

"Hi, guys," Keri sang as they went by.

"Hi," Cody said. He caught Ashley's eye. She was cold and unsmiling.

As the girls disappeared, Todd said, "Man, I see that girl in my dreams. It's always the same dream, too. I'm climbing a hill and Ashley is about ten feet ahead of me. I climb faster, but I never get any closer. Pretty soon I'm so out of breath that my chest aches like I'm having a heart attack. Then, suddenly, she stops. But when I move toward her, there's some kind of glass wall between us. I slam into it and bust my nose and I'm bleeding like crazy—and she's laughing."

"Sounds about right for a cold fish like Ashley," Cody said. "Wise up, man. Forget about her."

"Yeah, I know you're right," Todd admitted. "I just wish I could."

"Hey, look over there," Cody said, pointing to a long mound of leaves.

"Yeah. It doesn't look like the wind could have blown them like that," Todd said nervously.

Todd hung back, but Cody started to move toward the mound of leaves. On the way, he stumbled over beer cans and a broken golf club. Obviously, many people who passed through here had no respect for the environment. Whatever they didn't want anymore, they just tossed aside.

When Cody reached the mound, he kicked some of the leaves aside. Right away, he uncovered what looked like a large patch of newly turned earth.

"Come see this, Todd," Cody called out. "Someone's been digging here. It looks like these leaves were spread around to cover it up."

Chills ran down his spine. He had the sickening feeling that maybe he had found Freddy.

Chapter 6

"Oh, Cody, you don't think—" Todd said nervously. His eyes were big and frightened looking as he slowly walked over to join Cody by the mound.

Cody found a pointed stick and started to probe the soft dirt with it. It had rained about a week earlier and the earth was fairly soft. But this patch of soil had also been loosened recently, so the stick went in easily—too easily. When Cody hit something solid, he felt a sense of dread. He tried to swallow, but all the moisture in his mouth had suddenly dried up.

Todd stared at Cody. He said nothing.

Then Cody saw a bit of cloth beneath his stick. Red flannel. Both boys gasped.

They knew that Freddy had always worn an old red flannel shirt to bed.

"Call 911," Cody said. "I'll stay here."

The police came quickly and within a few minutes yellow crime-scene tape was strung around the orchard. Then more police cars arrived than Cody had ever seen in one place before.

Before midday, they pulled Freddy Paine from his shallow grave. The police weren't saying how he had died. That was for the coroner to determine later on.

But it was obvious that Freddy had been murdered. No one dies accidentally and then buries himself.

The police interviewed everybody at the rooming house. Cody insisted that he'd never seen Freddy high on anything. He said that Freddy had been a straight arrow in every respect.

Then Cody told the police officer about Red Breck. He said that after Red went into tenants' rooms, money and valuables often turned up missing.

"I'm not saying the guy is a thief, but just about everybody here has had stuff disappear," he said.

When Sgt. McCall finished taking Cody's statement, he went off to join the forensics people. They were in Freddy's room taking evidence in plastic bags. When they finished for the day, they left the yellow tape in place and said they'd be back the next morning.

Cody took Keri Alvarez downtown for tacos. He needed to get his mind off what had just happened.

"I feel just awful about Freddy," Keri said. "Poor little guy. He never hurt anybody. He was very sweet. It's so awful to know that somebody murdered him right there in the house!"

"Yeah. Breck and Denham are sticking to their story about Freddy being on drugs. They're saying that he might have been meeting his supplier out there in the orchard," Cody said. "But that's just nonsense."

"I wouldn't dare tell my parents what happened," Keri said. "Dad would be down here in two hours to pick me up! Cody, doesn't it give you the creeps to think that someone who lives with us might be a murderer?"

"I don't think any of us are in danger," Cody said. "Freddy must have gotten into a fight with somebody."

"Still, it makes me feel terrible," Keri went on. "That old house is spooky enough with the rafters and the floors creaking like it's cursed or something. I'd move out if there was anywhere else to go that was close to college."

"Have you talked to Ashley? What does she think?" Cody asked.

Keri was the only other roomer Ashley ever talked to. When Cody had seen Sgt. McCall talking to Ashley, she looked very unhappy.

"I don't think Ash is afraid of anything," Keri said. "She's just annoyed by all the fuss. She said nobody better try to mess with her because she's got a black belt in karate."

"She's an odd duck," Cody said. "She hates guys, but she dresses like she's auditioning for a show in Las Vegas."

"I don't understand it either," Keri said, still looking frightened by what had happened.

Keri looked so spooked that Cody tried to get her mind off the situation by talking about Ashley.

"How long have you known Ashley?" Cody asked. "I mean, I can't figure her out. She can't be as awful as she seems. Or can she?"

Keri shrugged. "I haven't known her all that long. She likes to hang out with me because I'm not as pretty as she is."

Cody snorted in disbelief. He'd never heard anything so outrageous. But Keri just smiled and said, "I'm not kidding. She told me that high school was ruined for her because one girl was even more beautiful than she was. But poor Ash is human—she has her problems, too."

Cody raised his eyebrows. "Yeah, what problems?" he asked. "Like bad hair days and maybe a zit or two popping out on her face at the wrong time?"

"Don't be cruel, Cody," Keri said gently. "Ashley's mom was a model. If you can believe it, she was even more beautiful than her daughter. Ashley says she was just *obsessed* with her looks. But then she kind of got old, you know."

"Happens in the best of families," Cody said dryly. "Unless you die young, you get old. Not much of a choice."

"Isn't that the truth?" Keri laughed. "But when Ashley's mom could no longer get work as a model, she got a job as a dancer in—you know, those cheap clubs. The guys who came there were really crude and insulting. Ashley sneaked in one night to see her mother dance. She heard men making horrible, degrading remarks to her mother. It broke her heart. She begged her mother to quit, but Ashley's father had skipped out, so she was stuck."

"Well, things must have turned out okay. Ashley is in college now. Her mom must be real proud that she's doing well," Cody said.

"No, it didn't turn out that way," Keri said, shaking her head sadly. "Her mother died when Ashley was 16. She had started using drugs to help her put up with those crummy jobs. One night she took too much. She just never woke up the next morning.

"Ashley sort of shrugs it off now. Sometimes she even kind of jokes about it. But I can see in her eyes that it hurt her bad. I think it *still* hurts her. That's why I try to put up with Ashley when she's being a pill. She's had her problems—"

"I guess," Cody said grudgingly. But he still couldn't feel any warmth toward the girl.

Keri sighed. "I'm so creeped out to think of going to bed in that house tonight. I wonder if he *died* in that room," she said, looking frightened again.

"Whoever killed Freddy had nothing to do with *you*, Keri. It had to be personal between the killer and Freddy," Cody said confidently.

But he didn't know that for sure. Anything was possible. In fact, Cody himself dreaded going back to the rooming house.

That night Cody read a novel until very late. Then he tried to sleep. But he didn't doze off until 2:00 A.M. All night he kept dreaming about Freddy Paine. In Cody's dream, Freddy was frantically trying to crawl out of his grave in the orchard.

Chapter 7

Cody and Todd left for work early the next morning.

"Old Breck is giving me some real dirty looks," Cody said. "I think he wishes I'd left poor little Freddy resting in peace under the leaves."

"Know what, Cody?" Todd said. "I was too scared to sleep, so I jammed a chair under the doorknob!"

"I don't blame you," Cody said. "We need to find another place to live."

"I guess this is what Breck was afraid would happen," Todd said. "Most everybody at the house is talking about moving out now. People are wondering who could be next."

"I've been thinking," Cody said.

"Maybe Denham killed Freddy. You know that guy gets really nasty when he's been drinking. Maybe he stumbled into Freddy's room by mistake. If Freddy thought he was a burglar, he could have attacked him or something."

"Could be. I just hope the cops hurry up and find out who did it. We'll all feel better when they take the murderer away," Todd said uneasily.

The coroner's report was released that day. It said that Freddy Paine's death had resulted from a sharp blow to the head. He'd suffered massive bleeding of the brain and died immediately.

Cody checked out other rooms for rent, but they were all too expensive. With so many college students scrambling for housing, it was easy for landlords to keep rents high. Only broken-down old rooming houses—some even worse than Breck's—charged what Cody could afford.

That Friday night, Cody was back in

his room, unable to sleep. He was listening to the weird, creaking noises the old house routinely made. Before Freddy's murder, those noises had never bothered him, but they did now.

Suddenly Cody heard footsteps coming down the hall. He recognized the unsteady, stumbling gait of a drunken Louis Denham. The guy was obviously coming in from another night of drinking. Cody felt sick. Maybe Denham had also drunkenly stumbled into Freddy's room that night. Maybe when Freddy confronted him, he'd lashed out like a madman.

Cody took a long, nervous breath. Then, to his horror, he realized that someone was trying to open his door!

It had to be Denham. As a former boxer, the man had a broken nose and a jagged scar on his chin that added to his generally brutish appearance. The thought of that ugly, drunken hulk forcing his way into this room made

Cody feel sick to his stomach.

Cody scrambled from his bed and grabbed a heavy metal flashlight. If Denham got in somehow, Cody planned to use the flashlight to defend himself.

Fumbling hands continued their efforts to open the door.

What did he want?

Maybe he *was* a madman. Freddy might not even have confronted him. Maybe he went into Freddy's room and killed him for no good reason at all!

Cody rushed to the closet and grabbed his old steel baseball bat. If he swung it at Denham's head, it would do a lot of damage. Cody stood alongside the door, planning to whack the intruder over the head the minute he came in. Then Cody would race into the hall and dial 911 on his cell phone.

Denham beat on the door with his hammy fists. "Archie, Archie!" he cried in a slurred voice. "You owe me 50 bucks! You know I loaned you a 50, Archie."

"Beat it, Denham!" Cody shouted through the locked door. "I'm not Archie, whoever he is. I'm Cody Walker! Go to bed right now, or I'll call the police!"

"They're coming over the ridge, Archie. I need the money. You hear me? They're coming over the ridge. There's a million of them, and they've got rifles, Archie. Give me my money now, you hear me?" Denham screamed.

Cody recognized that Denham was having what Grandmother called "DTs"— delirium tremens. This condition caused alcoholics to hear and see things that weren't there. Cody's grandmother tried to help guys like that when she found them sleeping out in the cold.

"Go away, Denham. I mean it. I'm getting the cops," Cody yelled.

Denham began kicking at the door and beating it with his fists. "They're coming, Archie. I got me a knife. I'll use it, too. I've done it before, Archie. Don't think you can cheat me again. You cheated me before, but you won't do it this time. I got me a knife, a big butcherman's knife, Archie—"

"I'm calling the cops right now!" Cody yelled. He cursed himself for leaving his cell phone on the nightstand. He was leaning against the door as Denham pushed from the other direction.

"You let me in my room *now*, Archie," Denham yelled. "You've got no business hanging out in my room."

"This is *my* room!" Cody shouted. "Your room is down the hall."

Then Cody heard another voice. "*Shhh!* You're waking up the whole house, Louie! The kids are complaining. You want to drive all my customers away? Why do you have to get so darned drunk? Ain't you got any sense? And what's that big knife for, answer me that!" Red Breck seemed almost gentle as he tried to quiet the other man down.

So Denham *did* have a knife! Cody shuddered at the thought of what might have happened if Denham had broken into his room.

"Don't be mad at me. Archie's in my room," Louis mumbled. "He won't give me my money. I won it in a crap game."

"Come on now. Off to bed with you," Red Breck said in a hoarse whisper. "You're scaring everybody. Do you know what's going to happen if this doesn't stop? They'll come get you and put you back where you were before. Think about it. You don't want that, Louie."

Denham began to sob loudly. Perspiration streamed from Cody's body as he heard the two men slowly move away from the door.

Chapter 8

Finally, Cody heard a door slamming shut at the end of the hall. Breathing a sigh of relief, he leaned on the door, the baseball bat still clutched in his hand. Maybe Denham really was confused about which room was his. Maybe he really did think that Cody's room was his. When a guy gets that drunk, he could easily get mixed up.

Or maybe it was more serious than that. It could be that Denham was actually a madman—and a murderer.

It was 2:00 A.M. now. Cody didn't even try to get back to sleep. He climbed back in bed and picked up the novel he was reading about two guys hiking through Alaska. Even though Cody wasn't a risk-taking guy himself, he enjoyed reading adventure stories.

When dawn came, Cody was glad to wolf down his oatmeal, swallow his black coffee, and get out of the rooming house. He knocked on Todd's door and shouted, "Come on, man. Time to go."

As they drove to work, Cody told his friend what had happened last night. "That Denham guy was trying to get into my room. Man, I freaked! At first, I thought he might have actually mistaken my room for his. But even if he had, he was acting really crazy, man—I mean like *dangerous* crazy! Maybe he freaked out the other night, too. And just maybe, he killed Freddy—"

Todd swallowed hard. "If we're this rattled, I bet the girls who live in the house are *really* scared!" he said.

"Keri is, but not Ashley. She's such an ice queen that nothing bothers her," Cody said.

Todd frowned at his friend's remark.

"You're awfully hard on her, Cody. She's probably had some bad experiences with guys. That must be why she's gun-shy. Who knows? She might turn into mush if a guy was to use the right approach."

Cody looked doubtful. "Dream on," he said.

Todd smiled. "You know those new gold chains at the store that she likes?"

Cody groaned. "Don't tell me you're going to try to bribe her!" he said. "Look, we're friends, Todd. I hate to see you get burned by that witch."

That evening, Cody and Keri went down to the coffee shop. It relaxed Cody to do something normal—like sitting around eating cheesecake and drinking coffee with a nice girl. It got his mind off the rooming house.

Even though he'd resolved to keep it to himself, Cody told Keri about Denham trying to get into his room. Her room was just down the hall. He thought she had the right to know.

"Oh, Cody!" Keri gasped. "That guy looks like a caveman or something! Why does Mr. Breck put up with him? I wonder if he ran a criminal check on that man before he decided to hire him."

"Old Denham may not have a criminal record," Cody said.

"I bet he does. Mr. Breck just doesn't care what happens to his tenants," Keri said bitterly.

Cody quickly changed the subject. "You won't believe this, Keri, but Todd is still having fantasies about dating Ashley. Is that incredible or what?" he said with a smile.

Keri laughed. "Guys really go for her. Even poor Freddy bought her perfume and a heart-shaped locket," she said. "But, of course, it was no deal."

"Todd is going to buy her a gold chain today," Cody said.

"Ashley will probably toss it in the trash. She sneered at Freddy's gold locket. It wasn't *real* gold, of course. She said Freddy probably got it as a prize in a box of cereal!" Keri said.

As Cody and Keri approached the rooming house, they saw police cars in the driveway.

"Oh, man, now what?" Cody groaned.

Keri gasped. "Do you think somebody else was murdered? I don't even want to look!" she cried as she buried her face in Cody's shoulder. "Last night I heard all kinds of terrible noises. I guess some of it must have been Denham trying to get in your room. That's probably what woke me up. But after that, I heard creepy sounds like moaning or something. Oh, Cody, I hope nothing bad has happened to Ashley. Wouldn't that be awful?"

"Hey, take it easy, Keri," Cody said reassuringly. "There are all kinds of reasons the cops might be here. Maybe somebody got in a fight. Or maybe Denham got drunk again and took a header down the stairs."

In spite of his own anxiety, it felt good

to have Keri in his arms. He stroked her back gently. Keri was a pretty cute girl, and nice, too. That was the main thing with him.

Keri finally got the courage to turn back toward the rooming house. She and Cody could both hear some kind of uproar going on inside. It sounded like the police were struggling to subdue somebody.

"Cody," Keri whispered, "can you tell what's going on?"

"I think so. It looks like they're taking somebody out," Cody said, straining to see. Then he saw two big police officers coming out the door of the rooming house. They were hauling a big writhing hulk between them.

Chapter 9

The police were leading a handcuffed Louis Denham across the porch and down the front steps.

"Oh, man!" Cody said. "The cops must have finally gotten the goods on Freddy's murderer. It was Denham!"

Red Breck was walking alongside, talking softly to the man in custody. Cody heard him say, "Don't worry, Louie. I'll get a lawyer on this right away and you'll be out of jail by tomorrow."

Denham was disheveled, and his eyes were wild. "I never hurt nobody in my life," he was saying. "*Never!* I didn't do anything. I'm being framed. It's a bum rap. Hey, I *liked* that little guy, Freddy. He kept his room up neat, and he was always real polite to me."

Ashley had stepped outside to get a better look. She walked over to join Cody and Keri when she saw them in the yard.

"Well, it looks like the big mystery has been solved," Ashley said. "Just look at that rotten excuse for a human being! It makes me sick to think a repulsive creature like Denham was living right down the hall from me!"

Denham was still struggling to get away. "Why won't anyone believe me? I swear that I'm innocent," he screamed as the officers put him in the back seat of the patrol car.

"The police must have a pretty good case against him, or they wouldn't be taking him away," Keri said.

Red Breck overheard Keri's comment and joined the group.

"It's not what you think," he said. "They found some old misdemeanor warrants on the guy, and *that's* what they're taking him in for. It's just drunk and disorderly stuff. Of course, they're hoping they can hang the murder on him too—but that's not going to fly."

Cody was surprised that Red Breck seemed distraught over Denham's arrest. He didn't think the hard-nosed house manager cared much about anybody.

"If he's innocent, they'll let him go," Cody said.

"They'd better!" Breck growled.

Now Cody was curious. "Is he a good friend of yours, Mr. Breck?" he asked.

"Yeah, you might say that. He's my half-brother. The two of us grew up together. He's not a bad guy. He's just had a lot of real tough breaks. I'll tell you this, though—when we were kids he was my hero. There was nothing he wouldn't do for me." Breck walked away, shaking his head and mumbling to himself.

Ashley sneered at him. "Yeah, right! I always knew that Breck was a stupid old geezer. *Obviously*, that freak Denham did it," she said.

"Red Breck isn't so old. He's only in

his late forties," Cody pointed out. "That doesn't exactly make him a geezer."

"So what? He's still a loser," Ashley snapped.

Cody looked into her deep, dark eyes. The girl was beautiful, all right. Cody knew where Todd was coming from. She might be the most beautiful girl Cody had ever seen. But right now she reminded him of a snake—a lovely coral snake with magnificent markings but an almost always fatal bite.

"You're a strange cat, Cody," Ashley continued in a cold, mean voice. "You defend old Breck, but you hate my guts, don't you?"

Cody was taken aback by the frank remark. But Keri cut in before he could say anything. "Oh, Ashley, Cody doesn't dislike you. He's just the kind of guy who speaks his mind."

Cody looked at Keri Alvarez. He'd been enjoying her company, but now he was disappointed. It seemed clear that while she was sweet, she didn't have a clue about the *real* world. She was one of those girls who can't stand for anybody's feelings to be hurt, so they live in their own little dreamland. Obviously, Keri was still caught up in childish fairy tales—except for the ugly characters like witches and ogres. Witches like Ashley.

Cody decided to speak out. "No, Ashley is right. I *don't* care much for her," he said. "I've never made a secret of that, have I, Ashley?"

"That's true," Ashley replied, not seeming to be at all offended. "So many guys make moves on me, it's kind of refreshing to meet somebody like you, Cody. Most of the time, men just slobber all over me. That makes me sick.

"But you know what, Cody? I once said you didn't stand a chance with me. I told you that you shouldn't even *try* to go there. Now I'm not so sure. You just might stand a chance after all."

Cody didn't hide his disgust. "Here's

some big news for you, Ashley," he said. "This guy is flat out not interested. Never was, never will be."

"Whoa!" Ashley said. "I *do* like you!"

"It's not mutual," Cody snapped.

Ashley slipped her hand in the crook of his arm. "Hey, big guy," she said in a flirty voice. "I dare you to go out for a soda with me. Then we'll see if you can resist my charms," she said with a gleam in her eye. "What have you got to lose?"

"Go on," Keri laughed. "Do it, Cody! I know I'm going to be proved right. You'll see. You'll discover that Ashley really does have a good side."

"Not interested," Cody repeated.

"Cody, Cody, Cody! You're afraid of me, aren't you?" Ashley taunted. "In fact you're so scared of me you don't even trust yourself! I dare you to come. I double dare you, chicken-boy."

Cody felt that he'd been backed into a corner. He glared at the girl. "You're on," he said, anger surging inside his veins.

Eager to get the "date" over with, Cody drove Ashley downtown to a small ice cream store. Cody ordered a chocolate soda for himself and a strawberry one for Ashley. Looking at her across the table, Cody had to admit something to himself. Ashley's perfectly gorgeous face and dynamite figure *were* pretty hard to resist. But good looks were simply not enough to make up for her personality.

"So, Cody, you don't have a steady girlfriend, right?" Ashley said. "I mean, I know you and that pathetic little twit, Keri, go out for coffee sometimes. But you guys aren't really *dating*, are you?"

"No, we're not. But Keri is not a pathetic little twit, and I like her a lot," Cody snapped.

"Poor baby," Ashley said. "Say—did I ever tell you about my mother?" Without waiting for Cody to answer, she rambled on. "Years ago she was one of the world's most beautiful models. Men fell all over themselves just to get a smile from her.

But then, you know, she couldn't find much modeling work as she got older. She had to become a dancer."

Cody didn't want to hear it. "Is that so?" he said with an exaggerated yawn.

Ashley's face hardened. "All the disgusting men made fun of her," she continued. "Poor Mommy. She kind of let herself go. But I'll *never* let myself go. I intend to stay as pretty as I am right now. I don't care how much I might have to spend on plastic surgery—I'll *never* be ugly! Come on, Cody, you're only human, aren't you? You're getting lost in my eyes—I can tell."

"No, I'm just enjoying my soda," Cody said.

Ashley didn't believe him. "Don't fight it!" she said with a confident smile. "Guys can't help going crazy over me. Just go with the flow, Cody. I promise you I won't be cruel. If you want to, you can even kiss me right now. I promise I won't slap your face."

Cody finished his soda and got up. "That's enough. This has been pretty boring, Ashley. See you around."

"Come back!" Ashley cried out as he walked away. Then, to Cody's surprise, she added, "You're a pretty cool guy, after all."

When Cody got back to the rooming house, most of the roomers were standing around talking about Denham's arrest. Denham was still sitting in the police car as the police finished up their paperwork. All the tension had left the scene. Everybody seemed deeply relieved that Freddy Paine's killer was now in custody.

Chapter 10

Finally, just as it got dark, the police took Denham away. The last handful of onlookers went inside.

Cody wondered about the evening Todd had planned. How would he make out when he tried to give Ashley the stupid gold chain? *Poor fool*, he thought to himself as he turned on the television to check out the local news.

"Police have arrested a handyman at the rooming house where college student Freddy Paine was found buried in an apple orchard," the news reporter said. "The suspect has not yet been charged with the murder. He is currently being held on unrelated charges. Paine was bludgeoned to death a week ago and later found in a shallow grave."

Cody called Keri to talk about the news flash he'd just heard. She answered after four rings. "I just walked in the door, Cody. Ashley and I went golfing. Gee, is she ever a whiz at the game! Man, I felt like such a doofus!"

After talking about Louis Denham's arrest for a few minutes, Keri rang off. She said she needed to shower and study for tomorrow's biology exam.

Suddenly, a strange thought popped into Cody's head. Several disconnected images were gradually beginning to form meaningful pictures. A creeping numbness spread over his body.

The broken golf club Cody found near Freddy's grave could well have been the murder weapon.

A golf club . . .

Cody jumped off the chair and hurried down the hall. He stopped at Todd's room and pounded on the door. There was no answer. That meant he'd already gone down to Ashley's room to give her his stupid gold chain.

Cody's heart was beating fast. He hesitated and tried to calm himself. *Maybe my idea is crazy*, he thought. *Maybe both of them will laugh at me.*

But Freddy Paine had tried to impress her with gifts, too—that gold locket and a bottle of perfume.

Cody remembered what he'd said to Todd. Not all dangerous psychos were hulking men with scarred faces and broken noses. Psychos come in all shapes and sizes.

Cody moved down the hall toward Ashley's room. As he approached her door, he could hear her angry voice. "I know what you *really* want, you pig!"

"Ashley, don't—*please don't*," Todd was whimpering.

Cody drew back from the door and then rushed at it with all his strength. The latch shattered and sprang open. Cody immediately saw Todd crouching in the corner. Blood was streaming from his forehead. Ashley was standing over him—a bloody golf club in her hands.

"He tried to attack me," Ashley cried.

"I *didn't!*" Todd wailed. "I just tried to give her a lousy gold chain!"

Todd was shaking and cowering. Tears were running down his cheeks. Cody had never seen such confusion and terror in a man.

Then Ashley started to go for Todd again. She raised the broken golf club high in the air. Her eyes were wild.

"You're a lying little weasel!" she screamed. "You're just like those lowlifes who destroyed my mother. You're nothing but a beast, and you deserve to die like one!"

Cody jumped between Ashley and Todd. "That's enough, Ash," he said in a calm voice. "Give me the golf club now. You've done enough damage. Come on, just hand it over."

A look of pure fury contorted the girl's beautiful face. Using both hands, she swung the golf club toward Cody's head. But Cody was too quick for her. After jumping aside, he grabbed her arms. Then he tried to wrench the weapon from her, but she wouldn't let go of it. Infuriated, she kicked Cody in the shins. An excruciating jolt of pain shot through his body.

As Cody writhed in pain, Ashley snatched the club away from him. Once again Cody tried to pull it away from her. He couldn't believe how strong she was. All that working out had made her stronger than most men twice her size.

"Help! Call 911!" Cody screamed to a frightened roomer who was peering in from the hall. "Get paramedics!"

Then Cody wrenched the golf club from the crazed girl, and this time he had it for good. But instead of admitting defeat, Ashley spun around and snatched a large vase off a table and brought it down hard on Cody's shoulder.

This time he didn't hesitate. In spite of

the pain he lunged forward, grabbing her upper arms and taking her down to the floor with him. She kept trying to kick at him as he struggled to hold onto her.

"Let me go! Let me go!" she screamed. "I didn't do anything but protect myself! Those rotten guys are responsible for what happened. They're all pigs. Like Paine. He called me into his room that night. He said he had a copy of the biology test and he'd share it with me. Of course, I'd be a fool to trust *any* man. So I took my golf club along with me, just in case. And sure enough—he tried to kiss me! The little creep tried to kiss me!"

When the police finally got there, it took two policewomen to subdue Ashley. She was yelling that Freddy and Todd had forced her to do what she did. It was self defense. Dealing with brutish men was the price every beautiful woman had to pay, she said. The same kind of men had gotten the best of her mother. So she'd built up her strength, Ashley went on. At just 16 years old, she'd stood by her mother's grave and sworn that no man would ever get the best of her. Not *ever*!

"What else could I do? They gave me no choice. Don't you see that none of this is my fault? I'm innocent!" Ashley wailed as they put her in the police car.

* * * *

At her trial several months later, Ashley was convicted of second-degree murder in the death of Freddy Paine. The members of the jury had deliberated for just one hour.

Cody was deeply affected by the whole affair. After the trial was over, he decided it was time to move on once again. As he was packing the last of his belongings, Todd came in his room. "So, buddy, have you decided where you're off to?" he asked.

"Yes, I have," he replied. "A little town up north with a good junior college. I'm off to be a bookhead!"

COMPREHENSION QUESTIONS

RECALLING DETAILS

1. What broken item in Freddy's room gave a clue to his disappearance?

2. Where was Freddy Paine's grave found?

3. What murder weapon did Cody find in the apple orchard?

IDENTIFYING CHARACTERS

1. Whose grandmother used to say that "beauty is as beauty does"?

2. Who was Red Breck's half-brother?

3. Whose mother had once been a beautiful model?

DRAWING CONCLUSIONS

1. Why did Ashley like to hang out with Keri Alvarez?

2. Why was Cody surprised that Freddy Paine had tried to date Ashley?

3. Why did Cody and Todd call the college students "bookheads"?